T0105537

FOND OF A
DOUBLE ENTENDRE

By

Cormac G. McDermott

Order this book online at www.trafford.com
or email orders@trafford.com

Most Trafford titles are also available at major online book retailers.

Printed in the United States of America.

ISBN: 978-1-4269-3813-9 (sc)
ISBN: 978-1-4269-3814-6 (e)

*Our mission is to efficiently provide the world's finest, most comprehensive book publishing
service, enabling every author to experience success. To find out how to publish your
book, your way, and have it available worldwide, visit us online at www.trafford.com*

Trafford rev. 7/12/2010

 www.trafford.com

North America & international
toll-free: 1 888 232 4444 (USA & Canada)
phone: 250 383 6864 ♦ fax: 812 355 4082

A girl friend of mine asked me 'do you put out your cat at night'...........I humorously replied 'when you want sex you 'put out' your cat at night also but, unlike the animal, yours is covered in a pair of lace knickers before doing so'!!

I learned during May 2010 that the playing surface at Wembley 'had been layed a number of times'...........I turned to one of the lads and quipped 'Lady Marmalade has been 'laid a number of times' also but if she was to have said 'voulez vous couchez avec moi ce soir' to one of the stadium's groundsmen they probably would have replied 'I bet ball was played with you before there was grass on the field you fecking brazer''!!

A person who helped in the process of publishing this book is called Josh Spears...........I felt like quipping 'does you uncle Chuck descend from zulus??'!!

I heard a member of the I.R.F.U. during May 2010 say that plans for the development of the Union had 'absolutely cracked'...........I thought 'a home boy in Los Angeles taking cocaine through a bong ends up being 'absolutely cracked' also but here in Dublin there is a rivalry between the northside and southside as opposed to between the eastside and westside I suppose'!!

I once sent a text to one of my mates asking him what time he had left the pub the previous night...........when he responded 'ten-ish'...........I quipped 'ten-ish??...........I suppose that's a game that involves racquets, balls and a net in Holland, ey??'!!

My girlfriend got one up on me one day when she said 'I have the wood on you'..........I hit back by retorting 'Pinocchio's wife giving him an erection while he's lying says 'the wood on you' also but at least I'll not ask to sit on your face like she 'wood"!!!!!

I have to laugh when I see black players playing for Dundee United, with a combination of skin tone and football gear........... I wonder what it would be like if they came up against a group of Umpa Lumpas playing for the All Blacks!!

Whilst listening to the radio one time I heard a deejay say, regarding winning a prize, that they would 'give away some room' in a hotel..........I figured 'when a 40 stone bloke gets off the DART he 'gives away some amount of room' also but at least the hotel doesn't stand a chance of derailing because of him'...........although the bottom could well fall out of the floor, ey?? !!

Entrepreneurs not wanting to open to markets in places like India and China makes as much sense as the makers of Vicks Nasal Spray telling Barry Manilow to keep his nose out of their business...........come to think of it they'd rather their business in his nose!!

A priest's clothing...........Prince's clothing...........and a black guy imitating Jesus...........aw yeah, 'Smoke On The Water' was recorded by Deep Purple!!

Here's some jokes poking fun at people's surnames............
please enjoy!!
Able: Ready, Willing And.......... is always there to lend a
helping hand!!
Acres: Green..........likes to pay the field!!
Alice : Who The F*ck Is.......... was a fan of Smokie!!
Angel: Heaven Must Be Missing An.......... was big into
Tavares!!
Attack: Panic..........suffers from anxiety depression!!

Some people were very surprised when George Michael
'came out' over a decade ago but I heard a story during
the Summer of 1990 that told me that he is not only as gay
as 'Last Christmas' but this Christmas, every Christmas
that's likely to come and the gobbling done by all the
pigeon-toed, leather-clad turkeys called Cecil in The Blue
Oyster on December 25th!!

My sister went to an opera called 'From The House Of
The Dead' which is set in Siberia ....I quipped 'when
a funeral director departs after burying the deceased he
leaves 'from the house of the dead' also but at least he has
a very small chance of bumping into a tiger who'd maul
him'!!

I got into an argument with a friend one day when he
told a guy in a wheelchair to get 'on his bike'..........I turned
and responded 'that's a terrible thing to say..........that's like
telling a thalidomide to get into his canoe'!!

Christy Moore obviously feels very hot when performing judging by the amount of sweating he does..........just put a pot under his scrotum and I guarantee you there would be enough water to hard boil his testicles..........and if you think a little more there would even be enough salt in the water to prevent the shells from cracking!!

I was in the pub one night having a discussion about football when one of the lads commented that Archie Knox, no matter where he went, would never get Rangers out of his blood..........I responded 'you're right, you'd have a better chance of getting Fort Knox, all the fried chicken and every blade of blue grass out of Kentucky unnoticed than getting Archie to lose his feelings for Reign Josh'!!

I see there is a young guy who plays for Man City called Weiss...........apparently his dad, Miami , wears even sharper suits than Jamie Redknapp!!

With the way Rafa Benitez gets his team to play the outcome really is a bit of a lottery..........it's like he's p*ssing into either a force nine gale where he gets his pants wet or if it's just the horse 'Breeze Out' standing with his ass facing him it looks like he's been ball juggling melting cod liver oil capsules which isn't so bad!!

Here's some more jokes about people's names...........

Bacon: Bringing Home The.........is a hardworking police officer!!
Bagg: Scum.........deals drugs!!
Bail: Cricket.........is forever getting stumped!!
Balding: Slowly.........has a receding hairline!!
Ball: Bowling.........actually likes to feel like a 'spare'!!
Bank: Deutsche.........sponsors classic golf tournaments!!
Bass: Pint Of......... pulls the odd gargle for Bertie Ahern in Fagan's, Drumcondra!!

I'm sure you are all aware of the 'bluetooth' mechanism on your mobile phones..........I often laugh to myself as if it had been invented by Roma gypsies it would have been called 'goldteeth'!!..........and if they had created McDonalds the golden arches would have had plaque on them!!

Why did a fight break out between Amir Khan and his masseur's genie??..........they both said they'd been rubbed up the wrong way!!

A friend of mine was getting broadband cheaply but never used it..........his response was 'EURO30 a month is not to be sniffed at'..........I retorted 'rat poison is not to be sniffed at but you don't realise your money goes down the drain even more quickly'!!

I see Ronseal Quick Dry Woodstain has the phrase 'it does exactly what it says on the tin'..........if that applied to Ace Lager they'd have to say 'drink too much of this stuff after eating barn brack and you'll lose at cards and puke your ring up'!!

…….…..and more jokes about names……….!!

Bastard: You Scouse………doesn't like being around Man U fans!!

Bath : Turkish………washes with the rest of his family!!

Batt: Cricket………is made of willow!!

Beach: Dollymount……….always has plenty of condoms on him!!

Bear: Bull And……….can be found at the stock exchange!!

Beard: Goatie………. doesn't have sideburns!!

Beaver: Eager………. never stops working!!

Beer: Lager………likes to have a few pints!!

Benjamin: Private………thinks she's Goldie Hawn!!

Benn: Big……….can be found in Westminster !!

Bill: Telephone………works for Eircom!!

Bing: Badda……….starred in Goodfellas!!

Binn: Dusty……….used to be the booby prize on 3-2-1!!

Birch: Silver……….can be found in forests!!

Bird: Free As A……….helped John Lennon write songs!!

Birdseye: Captain……….goes around growling 'H'har har, would ya like some fish fingers?'!!

Bishop: Bash The……….is forever chastising Chita !!

Black: In The……….has a very healthy bank balance!!

Blight: Potato……….forced Irish people to emigrate to the U.S.!!.

Bolt: Lightning………. helped U2 record 'Electrical Storm'!!

Bound: House……….gets snowed-in regularly!!

Bone: Funny……….is always cracking jokes!!

Boot: Car……….frequently has bric-a-brac sales!!

Somebody once said to me 'did you know Aberdeen is called 'Furry Boots City'..........I added 'given the footwear a lot of Dublin women don this could be called 'furry boots city' also but at least Dubs are not afraid to break into a penny'!!!!!

I was sitting having a pint with some friends one night when one of them said that a girl whom I've never fancied was looking really great..........I retorted 'she wouldn't get a kiss if she was The Blarney Stone dressed up as Pamela Anderson'!!!!!

Booth: Telephone..........is always having his glass smashed!!
Bottom: Rock.......... just got laid off from work!!
Bowler: Spin..........appeals like Monty Panesar!!
Box: Jack In The..........pops up out of nowhere!!
Boyle: Hard.......... doesn't like soft yokes!!
Brake: Front..........always flies over the handle-bars!!
Branch: Special..........hunts down criminals!!
Breeze: Cool As A.......... never gets flustered!!

I was watching Gillette Soccer Saturday over the 2009 Xmas period and have never seen so much arguing..........
if a frightened Irish skunk, dressed as a suicide bomber, drinking whiskey and launching stink bombs from it's ass walked in and ordered 'next year's World Cup better be held in Afghanistan' there couldn't have been more consternation!!

I stopped at a petrol station with a friend of mine, whom I asked to put some unleaded fuel into my car.........when I asked him if he had done so he replied 'I actually put some leaded in'.........needless to say I freaked.........his response was 'I only pumped some lead into the car, it'll still be able to run'............I jokingly said 'JFK had some lead pumped into him and he wasn't even able to run for cover let alone for President of the United States again'!!!!!

Brian: Life Of.......... likes to look on the bright side of life!!

Bridge: London..........is falling down, falling down, falling down!!

Brother: He Ain't Heavy, He's My..........has a collection of The Hollies music!!

Budd: Nipped In The..........doesn't leave anything to chance!!

Bush: A Bird In The Hand Is Worth Two In The.......... is happy with his lot!!

Buss: Dublin..........works the Nitelink!!

Butcher: Pork..........brings home the bacon!!

Butt: Head..........tries to imitate Zinedine Zidane's antics from the 2006 World Cup Final!!

Cage: Bird..........is full of sandpaper and seed!!

Cake: Birthday..........has lots of candles stuck in him!!

Canter: Wins In A..........scores lots of goals!!

Cheek: Tongue In..........likes to poke fun at people!!

Cheese: Blue Vein..........goes well with crackers!!

Chick: Dixie..........is from the American mid-west!!

Christian: Born Again..........acts like Glenn Hoddle and Sir Cliff Richard!!

Church: Unraptured..........is ready to disappear 'in the twinkling of an eye'!!

Clerk: Insurance..........arranges life and car policies!!

Close: Brookside..........made up ground-breaking story lines!!

Comfort: Southern.........goes well with red lemonade!!

Cook: Ready Steady.........appears as a chef on the B.B.C.!!

Coombe: Biddy Mulligan The Bride Of The.........is down in Dublin folklore!!

Coote: Bald As A..........wears a sypup!!

Cosh: Under The.........practices karate after repressing his lady friend!!

Couch: Casting.........slept her way to the top!!

Court: Tennis.........gets tram lines done when having his head shaved!!

Crabb: Alaskan King..........is found in restaurants!!

Crapp: Cut The..........doesn't stand for any nonsense!!

Crew: The Cookie.........wanted us to 'Rock Da House' back in the early Nineties!!

Crisp: Clean And...........walks in freshly fallen snow!!

Crop: Cream Of The..........excels at everything he does!!

I was watching football with a girl I really fancy when the co-commentator said, on seeing a fierce challenge between two opposing players that angered both of them, that it was 'a full-blooded committed tackle'..........I turned to her and said sexily 'if you were kind enough to give me an erection, you'd have a full-blooded committed tackle also but far from confronting you I'd let you tickle the bottom of my scrotum aswell'!!!!!

Cross: Sutton..........doesn't know which side of the Hill Of Howth to go to!!

Cuff: The Collars Don't Match The..........is a brunette who dyes her hair blonde!!

Curley: Short And.........makes aphro combs!!

Cutt: Hair...........is a barber by trade!!

Deal: Real..........is a football agent for Madrid!!

Derby : Donkey.........rides along the beach with an ice cream!!

I was watching Coventry City play Portsmouth in an F.A. Cup third round replay during January 2010 when I spotted that the Sky Blues had a Wood, Eastwood and Westwood playing for them..........all we needed was for Park Ji Sung, whom the Man U fans call 'Tree Lungs', to come on and we'd have been able to repair the damage done to the Rain Forests Of South America!!

Diddle: Hey Diddle.........jumped over the moon with a cow!!

Dock: Hickory Dickory..........saw a mouse run up the clock!!

Doe: Ah Buh Dee Doo Doh Don't Dee..........played a Scouser in Harry Enfield!!

Dover : Ben...........likes tying his shoe laces!!

Down: Up...........is a very confused G.A.A. fan from Ulster !!

Driver: Taxi.........reckoned that de-regulation was a disaster!!

Duck: Peking.........is served up in my local Chinese take away!!

Dummer: Dumb And.........have a company called 'I Got Worms'!!

Eden : East Of.........came back from the dead!!
Everest: Mount.........got mounted by Chris Bonnington..........and his jar of Bovril!!
Eye: An Eye For An.........seeks revenge!!
Fair: Scarborough.........wants to know where you are going!!
Farthing: Penny.........gets on her bike!!
Farewell: Fond.........left behind those who loved him!!
Feather: Birds Of A..........is always around those whom she's like!!
Field: Ann..........is full of Liverpool supporters!!
Fine: I Feel.........told The Beatles she's in love with him!!
Finn: Huckleberry..........has lots of friends!!

I once heard a group of girls saying they were going out to 'hit the tiles'..........I turned and said 'after a few pints I'm so drunk my piddle gets ready to hit the tiles also but at least you have no chance of catching your flute in a zip'!!!!!

Fisk: Nil............makes vacuum cleaners!!
Fitter: Carpet.........spends a lot of time on his knees!!
Fitz-gibbon: Randy........... is the Irish-American who brought AIDS into the world!!
Flag: Flying The.........takes part in the opening ceremony of the Olympics!!
Flask: Hip.........is full of Paddy whiskey!!
Flash: Quick As A..........can run the 100 metres in less than 10 seconds!!

I broke my leg playing football against a soccer club in Dublin called Cherry Orchard when I was a teenager, when on going for a medical for the Green Card to the United States, the doctor on feeling my leg asked where it had been broken..........now I've always felt a little intimidated by the middle class and nervously answered 'Ballyfermot'........... needless to say the man found this highly amusing!!

I was in school and got into trouble for laughing at a teacher when I was sent to see the form-master..........one of my class-mates asked if I managed to keep a straight face..........I quipped 'you must be joking, I was like a fish who had been caught by an angler's hook while suffering from Bell's palsy after having a stroke when doing an Elvis impression'!!!!!

One time I went to an Aslan concert in Finglas when a friend of mine asked if it was 'an eye-opener'..........I humorously answered 'a lap dancer with Bell's palsy is an eye-opener but at least she'll offer you the king of 'crack' that would blow your mind for the right reasons'!!!!!

I was eating a bag of Manhattan one night in the pub when one of my mates asked 'are you not watching your cholesterol, they're a silent killer'..........I retorted 'if you were to cheat with Marcel Marceau's wife while he was holding a Colt 45, you'd be dealing with a silent killer also but at least he'd have had an excuse for being angry at somebody licking 'nuts'!!!!!

Foot: Athletes..........has itchy toes!!

Forest: Nottingham..........plays football at The City Ground!!

Forty: Life Begins At..........enjoys every day!!

Forward: Fast..........is impatient with some things he sees on dvd!!

Fox: Sly..........wants you to all the way with him!!

Friend: Pen..........likes to write letters!!

Furnace: Firey..........melts metals!!

Gabb: Gift Of The..........never stops talking!!

Gabriel: The Angel..........appeared to Mohammed over two decades!!

Gale: Force 9..........bends over after eating a tin of beans!!

Gains: Capital..........had a type of tax named after him!!

Game: The Sunday..........is presented by Michael Lyster!!

Gate: St. James's..........visits the Guinness factory!!

Gates: Pearly..........bumped into a bouncer called St. Peter!!

Gell: Hair..........likes to style his 'barnet'!!

Gentle: Soft And..........makes toiletries!!

Gentleman: An Officer And A..........put Richard Gere in uniform!!

George: Cross Of Saint..........is found plentifully at England international soccer games!!

Getty: Spa..........goes well with Bolognese sauce!!

Gilder: Dutch..........bought lots of tulips before the introduction of the 'euro zone'!!

Gill: Darby O'..........drank with the 'little people'!!

Ginn: Tonic And..........sends people into depression!!

Glass: Heart Of..........was found out by Deborah Harry!!

Glew: Pot Of..........sticks to his guns!!

Grant: Student..........goes on the tap after receiving his twice yearly cheque!!

I was watching boxing one time when a guy threw a low blow..........my friend said 'that was a bad jab'..........I responded 'the guy who administered the MMR vaccine made a bad jab also but at least he deserved to have the b*llix knocked out of him'!!!!!

I was having a discussion with a girl I once knew when she remarked that she didn't understand why I found the title of the film 'Free Willy' a little embarrassing..........I looked her in the eye and said firmly 'how would you like it if there was a flick called 'Pussy On The Cheap''!!!!!

I often think that it is a good thing that Stevie Wonder and Gabrielle aren't cleptomaniacs because, if they were down to their last few quid, she'd rob him blind and he'd take the eye out of her head!!!!!

A prisoner did a crap in his chamber pot and asked the prison guard to empty it..........he responded 'you'll have to wait until tomorrow'..........the prisoner angrily retorted 'it's porridge I'm meant to be doing not Coco Pops'!!!!! Ughh..........just visualise it a little!!

Here's one that was written after the first time a game of football had been broadcast in 3-d at the end of January 2010 between Arsenal and Man U!!

As for this 3-d (i.e. thrupenny bit) game, it's the closest Awssnoh will come to contesting anything to do with metal this season and thrupence is what the Glazers were worth when Sir Alex Ferguson was sh*tting his nappy!!

I see Portsmouth F.C. were served a winding up order..........I thought to myself 'when I demanded that my friend Spiral tell me Billy Connolly's joke about cuckoo clocks, that was a winding up order also but at least I didn't have to pay millions of pounds to Her Majesty's Revenue & Customs'!!!!!

Here are a couple of jokes which were written the day after Super Bowl XLIV which was played on February 7th 2010!!

What's the difference between Peyton Manning and the North Strand here in Dublin during WWII??..........at least the North Strand could deal with a blitz!!

Would somebody please tell me if Super Bowl XLIV was played in Harlem as opposed to south Florida as some white guy i.e. Peyton Manning, with leather in his hand coming out of the pocket was set upon by a group of big black guys who probably thought it was his wallet!!!!!

I was talking to an old friend of mine who told me he gave up smoking cannabis as, to quote him, 'he came close to being stoned'..........I humorously replied 'Mary Magdelene came close to being stoned also but the only bit of blow that touched her lips is when she was giving oral sex'!!!!!

I got a part one time as an extra on a film that was being shot in a pub...........a jealous person I knew said begrudgingly 'it was only a cameo role'..........I replied 'when Larry Blackmon took off his cod-piece and checked himself for testicular cancer that was just a 'Cameo roll' also but at least I got several pints of beer for free'!!

I was in the pub one night when a friend of mine, with a few drinks on him, said 'greatest tits' instead of 'greatest hits'..........one of the lads reacted 'that's a Freudian slip'..........I continued 'a Freudian slip is what Sigmund's wife put on beneath her dress also but at least you're obviously able to have some fun while drunk'!!!!!

One day I asked a friend of mine what he had bought in the pharmacy when he turned and said 'French tickler' condoms..........I responded 'David Ginola playing with his children is a French tickler also but at least his kids have ribs for their own pleasure'!!!!!

I was having a discussion about my beloved Liverpool overcoming Roma in Rome in 1984 to win the European Cup when my friend said 'yeah, they were beaten in their own back yard'..........I humorously added 'when Harold Steptoe flogged Hercules for next to nothing he was beaten in his own back yard by his father also but at least the Scousers only wet their pants because they were laughing so much'!!!!!

Everton fans think they are great when they wind us Reds up by saying that they are 'The People's club' but because they make 'tits' of themselves after going out of every 'cup' competition they should really be called 'The Page 3 of The Sun's club'............and we all know what a 'flop' that newspaper is on Merseyside!!!!!

The Republic Of Ireland had a game during May 2010 that I heard a deejay say was 'a behind closed doors affair'..........I turned to my dad and said 'John Profumo had 'a behind closed doors affair' also but at least a game of football will not threaten to bring down the government..........unless the Taoiseach happened to be involved in a betting 'Scandal' of some sort that is'!!

A deejay at Dublin's 98 once asked listeners to text in the strangest things they had eaten as a child..........here's what I said..........'Hi Dec, when I was 5 I ate either Whiskas or Kite Kat while visiting my relatives in Birmingham.......... let's just say I spent the next while checking to see if my arseh*le was surrounded by fur'!!!!!

I was watching Adam Boulton on Sky News one Sunday morning when he mentioned something about a 'fringe party' in politics..........I turned to my girlfriend and said 'when Jim Carey was telling jokes in 'Dumb & Dumber' that, because of his hair, was a 'fringe party' also but at least Adam doesn't bother people about shrimps on barbies'!!!!!

..........and in relation to the above Mr. Boulton alluded to a 'bean party'..........I continued to my partner 'there was a 'bean party' in 'Blazing Saddles' also but at least in politics the hot air came out of their mouths as opposed to their asses'!!!!!

It always makes me laugh when I hear people say 'the greatest thing since sliced bread'...........I have to say I disagree............the reason being bread doesn't slice itself............they should say 'the greatest thing since the implement that slices the bread in the first place was created'!!

I was told a joke once that was even funnier than Gabrielle's glass eye, which was checking out zebras, smashing through her inch thick monicle into a jar full of Everton toffee and bullseyes!!

An old friend of mine contracted Bell's palsy one Xmas and told me that his doctors gave him special tape to keep his eye shut while trying to sleep...........I felt like saying 'could you not have used that tape to help wrap a box of sleeping pills as a present for yourself??!!!!!

I heard a deejay once say, as we were entering Spring, that there was 'a stretch in the evenings'...........I turned to my sister and said 'when our brother-in-law, who works nights, gets out of bed he has 'a stretch in the evenings' also but I bet that deejay's bed is made before he leaves for work'!!!!!

A friend of mine got some phlegm caught while talking one day when I said 'you've a frog caught in your throat'..........I continued 'when Kermit and Eric Cantona French kiss you could say there is a Frog in somebody's throat also but at least when you cough up phlegm it doesn't talk about seagulls following trawlers'!!!!!

I heard a deejay say that he 'had a hunch' that a song he played would be one of the songs of the Summer of 2010..........I thought to myself 'Notre Dame Cathedral 'had a Hunch' also but at least the recording artist probably smoked a Camel as opposed to looking like one'!!

Here's one that was written during May 2010 when there was a series of advertisements regarding the below!!

Goodfellas may be the only pizza recommended by the pizza 'fairy' but apparently they are going to face stiff competition from gay rivals Quare-fellas who are very much aware of where they can stick their pepperonis.......... and they actually recommend this to the pizza fairy himself!!

On reading one of my books a friend of mine called me a 'fruit loop'..........I retorted 'when Elton John said that Jesus Christ was gay he was a 'fruit' loop also but at least my plum is just a plum and not a passion fruit'!!!!!

A friend of mine once said that 'those fruit machines are addictive'..........I quipped 'a guy who continuously rents male prostitutes is addicted to 'fruit machines' also but at least when you spend your money in an arcade you've no chance of contracting HIV'!!!!!

One day I hit my elbow and began to ooh and aah out of me..........my dad said 'that's the funny bone tingling'..........I responded 'when Ashley Cole was pictured naked that was a funny bone that made women tingle also but at least hitting your humerus would not cost you your marriage to Cheryl Tweedy'!!!!!

A friend of mine said 'we should go to Disneyland, it's a fun city'..........I replied ' Liverpool is a fun city but at least the Mickey Mousers there are 'real' people'!!!!!

My dad was watching a dvd one night when I asked him what he was looking at..........he said 'From Russia With Love'............I humorously responded 'when CSKA Moscow play away from home in the Champions League they travel 'from Russia with Wagner Love' but at least Sean Connery didn't have his hair tied up in ridiculous looking dreadlocks'!!

I heard Marty Whelan say on an ad on the radio for Spar that 'you can eat it but won't beat it'..........I thought 'you can eat but not beat an Easter egg but at least The Easter Bunny doesn't appear on the cover of Playboy'!!

I had a birthday where the party-goers were just informed about it by word of mouth..........one of my friends wasn't told directly by me and complained that 'he had been left out in the cold'.............I said 'when Winter time comes around the milk bottles are left out in the cold also but at least they don't wait around moaning for invites through the post'!!!!!

One of my friends possessed what he thought was a counterfeit 50 euro note which he said was 'funny money'..........I quipped 'Dr. Creflo 'Dollar' (from The GOD Channel) telling jokes is 'funny money' also but at least he doesn't threaten to bring down the European Central Bank'!!!!!

I saw that there was a player who played for Swindon Town in 2010 with the surname 'Austin'..........I turned to my dad and laughed 'apparently his brother Earth Calling used to say 'nanu nanu' in Mork & Mindy'!!

I once knew a girl who was even more 'horny' than a sex-starved Satan's pet rhinocerus!!!!!

My sister spotted a big car one day that she commented was a 'gas guzzler'...........I replied 'people sucking helium out of balloons are 'gas guzzlers' also but at least when you talk after getting out of your vehicle you'd not sound like you were kicked in the fun and frolics'!!!!!

A friend of mine told me he and his wife had a argument after she refused to put on his Brazilian football jersey in order to turn him on before sex...........I said 'so you got off your bike (i.e. got angry), ey'...........I continued 'don't feel too guilty as Lance Armstrong has got off his bike on a few occasions but at least he'd no problem wearing a yellow jersey'!!

I see the head coach of the Irish rugby union team was called Declan Kidney...........apparently his brother, Steak And, is as nice as pie!!

My dad one day said 'did you know alcohol is called 'giggle water''.............I responded 'when I listen to my Billy Connolly tape, because I wet myself, that could be called giggle water also but at least when you have a bev you go on the p*ss instead of smelling like it'!!!!!

A friend of mine one day said that a guy we knew was 'a bit mad'...........I added 'the poor unfortunate gobshite, even if he won the Euro Millions he wouldn't be able to buy himself the full shilling'!!!!!

My friend once told some jokes that another commented 'went down like lead balloons'...........I quipped 'Katie Price jumping out of the Hindenburg went down like lead 'balloons' also but at least that didn't make the glamour model lose her sense of humour'!!!!!

Another friend of mine once drank some cans of cheap lager which made him feel unwell so he left the room holding his stomach...........one of the lads said 'he's going for the big spit' i.e. to vomit..........I said 'El Hadji Diouf always seems to go for the big spit also but at least when Whacker plays football he doesn't wipe his snots on his sleave'!!!!!

Here's one that was written during the episode where there was tension between John Terry and Wayne Bridge after the former's alleged affair with the latter's ex-girlfriend at the end of February 2010!!

Some player was quoted in one of the English tabloids as saying Wayne Bridge was a 'bottler'...........I turned to my sister and commented 'Brendan Grace has been known to be a Bottler on occasions also but at least Wayne has never said 'free a nipper, free a nipper...........RIGHT'!!!!!

I was in the gym one night when, on lifting some weights, my friend said 'you're going for the burn'..........I responded 'the son of perdition is going for the burn also when he's fecked into Hell but at least I'm not a liar and a deceiver'!!!!!

While watching 'Escape From Alcatraz' with my dad when I was a child I asked him what was going on..........he replied 'they're trying to go over the wall'..........I said 'every time David Beckham took a free kick he tried to go over the wall also but at least it wasn't because he was shagged up the arse each time he had a shower with the lads'!!!!!

It always makes me laugh when I see football clubs with the word 'Sporting' in their name..........of course they are going to say they are 'sporting'..........they're hardly going to call themselves 'We Are A Shower Of Dirty, Cheating B*stards Lisbon' for example now are they??!!!!!

I was watching 'Gladiators' on television one evening when my girlfriend said 'that greasy pole is good fun, ey'..........I humorously replied 'Pope John Paul II working in Macari's take-away would be a 'greasy Pole' also but at least those Gladiators don't have to say a funeral mass when 'Another One Bites The Dust'!!!!!

I was watching the news when there was something mentioned about the 'Green Belt' surrounding Dublin Airport..........I though to myself 'a novice in karate wears a green belt also but at least the area around the airport doesn't aspire to go around breaking people up like Bruce Lee'!!!!!

My dad once said to me that gardeners had 'green fingers'..........I replied 'Kermit The Frog washing his hands in Swarfega has green fingers also but at least Mellors was never hen-pecked by a pig!!

I was at a pub quiz when we had difficulty answering a question...........my cousin said 'you should just have a stab in the dark'..........I humorously retorted 'if I wanted a stab in the dark I'd wear a Rangers jersey in Limerick city after 10 p.m.'!!!!!

Here's one I wrote during the period where there was a lot of displeasure among the Man Utd fans regarding how the Glazer family were getting their club further into the red...........it was written at the beginning of March 2010!!
What's the difference between Man Utd and Bank Of Ireland, College Green??.....at least if Bank Of Ireland , College Green got 'the glazers' in they wouldn't end up hundreds of millions in debt!!

My uncle was hiding some money away from his wife when he said 'he was putting it in his 'grouch bag'..........I thought 'Eamon Dunphy being refused entry to a nightclub could be referred to as a 'grouch bag' also but at least he's probably not afraid of what his other half knows about his finances'!!!!!

I once heard a smug female boast that she had a job in 'asset management'..........I felt like retorting 'my partner has melon boobs and, because she knows when to flaunt them, she has great 'asset management' also but not even a subscription for 10 million euros would give you a horn like a sex-starved unicorn on Viagra'!!!!!

People in Dublin have become very proud ever since the Celtic Tiger..........it really did become a case of keeping up with the Jones's...........even the pitbulls will only urinate in public if it's up against gold plated lamp-poles!!!!!

I once heard Andy Gray say that a shot on goal 'went straight down the goalkeepers throat'.............I thought to myself 'a spoonful of Benylin goes straight down the throat also but at least, unlike when you go for the medical for the Green Card, when you cough you don't have your balls felt'!!!!!

My dad once told me that when you take a risk regarding something you 'hang it out'..........I responded 'homosexuals in Baghdad in that case 'hang it out' also but when they get caught they themselves are hung out..........at least you don't have to worry about hanging arse-less jeans out on the washing line though'!!!!!

I read on Ceefax during May 2010 that a footballer 'had got cramp in the first leg of a play-off'..........I turned to one of the lads and said 'surely he got cramp in either his right or left leg'!!

Here's one that was written during the period when Man Utd fans had their green and gold protest against their American owners…………..it was thought up during mid-March 2010!! The initials of the colours of the rainbow are R.O.Y.G.B.I.V...........now if the owner of Man Utd is a leprechaun his money is in a crock of gold at it's end..........and believe me 'crock' is the operative word because these initials stand for 'Running Of Yank Glazer's Business Is Vacuous'!!!!!

Here's another one that was written during the period when Liverpool fans were disgruntled at the fact that there seemed to be no movement in the building of their new stadium.......... it was written during the middle of March 2010!!

Because Liverpool have just the foundations layed for our new stadium it should be named 'Bedrock'..........Hicks and Gillett can 'Walk The Dinosaur' as it's a case of 'WAS Not WAS' i.e. 'Where's Ah Stadium Not Winners Are Scousers'

..........and to the tune of this song!!

'Doom, gloom,
Funds are lackin' Yank fools.
Doom, gloom,
Funds are lackin',
Whack, they're fools'!!!!!

My late mother told me that U.S. politicians call the place of Congress 'The Hill'..........I thought 'Dublin G.A.A. fans call their place of congregation 'The Hill' also but at least politicians in the U.S. get voted in by Californians as opposed to being abused by Tallaght-fornians'!!!!!

A girl I know once described me as her 'huggy bear'..........I quipped 'Starsky & Hutch had a Huggy Bear also but at least my bottom lip doesn't look like it was caught in a tug-o'-war'!!

My friend once asked did I know The Beatles had a song called 'I Am The Walrus'..........I replied 'Craig Stadler could proclaim to be The Walrus also but at least his golfing attire wasn't as ridiculous as that in Magical Mystery Tour'!!!!!

I was watching Sky News one day when they said, regarding a crime issue, the police were 'following leads'...........I turned to my dad and quipped 'the blokes who click through the turnstiles every fortnight at Elland Road 'follow Leeds' also but at least it's only the policeman's dogs, and not the ball players, who 'Bite Yer Legs'!!

I once heard a rapper describe something cool as being 'in da house'...........I thought to myself 'Big Brother is filmed 'in da house' also but I suppose most rappers are not sensationalistic 'dizzee rascals'!!

I was also asked if I knew that Neil Kinnock was nicknamed 'The Welsh Windbag'...........I responded 'Ryan Giggs sitting on a whoopie cushion in Cardiff could be referred to as a 'Welsh windbag' also but at least he's not afraid to come in off the 'left wing' on the odd occasion'!!

I heard Bobby Zamora say on Sky Sports News during April 2010 that, as far as trying to get into England's World Cup squad, he'd 'crack on'...........I turned to my girlfriend and cheekily quipped 'when you're in control of the bedroom after making yourself an omelette it's 'crack on' also but at least the Fulham striker cannot be replaced by a blow up doll'!!

I was listening to the radio when I heard the song 'I Ain't Gonna Bump No More' played..........I thought 'a woman who has had a hysterectomy 'ain't gonna bump no more' either but seldom when you listen to a song would you feel the liberty to ride like the clappers'!!

I wrote a piece regarding why I thought we were about to enter the era of the antichrist which my friend described as being 'deep sh*t'..........I retorted 'a slurry pit is 'deep sh*t' also but at least I'm not going to practice Sodomy'!!

The publishers of my books told me that the receipt of my free copies I get with my package were 'in the pipeline'..........I thought 'oil coming out of Iraq is 'in the pipeline' also but at least my books are a 'barrel' of laughs and don't cost $100 each'!!

I was asked one day if I knew that the nickname for Jamaica is 'Jamdung'..........I quipped 'Martin Chivers having a crap is 'jam dung' also but at least he's not afraid of anything that's taxing'!!

Apparently Goldie Hawn has a Spanish relative called Sporting Hee who wanted to bring Ruud Van Nistelrooy to La Primera Liga prior to the introduction of the euro so he could pay him in pes-HAY-tas!!!!!

I heard on Sky News that when soldiers in Helmand province in Afghanistan heard the sound of guns coming from their barracks that they regarded it as just 'friendly fire'..........I turned to my dad and said 'when Maguire & Patterson brought out safety matches they maintained it was 'friendly fire' also but at least they didn't have to deal with the potential of encountering suicide bombers'!!!!!

Somebody once described to me that the majority of the people of rural Ireland live 'in the sticks'..........I humorously responded 'one of The Three Little Pigs, who built his house out of wood, housing Peter Crouch and Niall Quinn is 'in the sticks' also but at least the people of rural Ireland don't have sangiches of hang made out of them'!!

It always makes me laugh when I hear football clubs say that they want to 'put bums on seats'..........well I tell yiz, if all they put on seats were 'bums' they'd make no money as all they'd do is mooch off each other for the price of a single cup of Bovril!!!!!

I once heard a guy who knew a businessman whom he described 'jet sets'..........I replied 'Roger Federer flying through a game of tennis 'jet sets' also but I doubt he encounters any air hostesses who want to give him some 'love deuce'!!

I had a discussion with a fellow Liverpool fan who said, about a player who had still to prove himself, that the 'jury is out' on him..........I thought 'when I watched Wimbledon some years back Joe 'Jury was out' on a few occasions also but at least she was happy to be in the 'court'!!

While sipping his first pint for a while my friend said 'it's just what the doctor ordered'..........I quipped 'when I played football at U.C.D. Tony O'Neill made me do sit ups I didn't want to do which was 'just what the doctor ordered' also but in fairness to the man at least I never had to put my hand in my pocket for a drink'!!

I was watching football one day when I heard the commentator describe a team, who had fallen four goals behind, as having the 'proverbial mountain to climb'..........I thought 'a fly at the foot of a dung heap has the 'proverbial mountain' to climb also but at least, unlike the conceding goalkeeper, a fly cannot be himself described as a heap of sh*te'!!

I was also watching the Press Preview on Sky News which the presenter said was 'still to come'..........I thought to myself 'a one year old has 'still to come' also but I suppose if they were to have tried to have turned to Page 3 of The Sun at least the pages wouldn't be stuck together'!!

I once told a racist joke which my sister told me wasn't 'politically correct'..........I retorted 'when I enlightened Barack Obama as to the corruption within the Federal Reserve that was a 'political correction' also but I suppose I shouldn't have followed it up by calling them mother f*ckin' hustlas'!!

I saw on the teletext one day that Fernando Torres said about Liverpool that 'the best is yet to come'...........well I have to say I disagree because if Calum is anything like his father, Georgie, he'd have lost his virginity a long time ago!!

Walter Smith said at the end of March 2010 that a supporters trust taking over at Reign Josh was 'worth having a look at'..........I thought 'a calendar of Kelly Brook is 'worth having a look at' also but I suppose she's not deluded enough to believe that 'We Are The People'!!

During the middle of March 2010 there was trouble in Clontarf on Dublin's northside when a head shop opened which somebody described as being 'a recipe for disaster'............I quipped 'getting Delia Smith on the board at Norwich City was obviously a 'recipe for disaster' also which, on relegation to the first division, made them all have Canaries'!!

I always laugh at the prospect of the following headline 'New York Giants Hit Browns In Bowl' because all you would have to do is move the first 's' to link up with the next word and you would have 'New York Giant Shit Browns In Bowl'!! Ughh!!

While also walking home from town during Easter week a person asked me where Summerhill was..........I quipped 'I can only tell you where 'Spring'hill is..........come back to me during June or July and I'll be able to enlighten you........... but don't ever ask me where 'Winter'hill is because I'll be snowed under'!!!!!

My dad bought an electrical appliance which he discovered was 'faulty'...........I quipped 'Basil and Cybil could be referred to as being 'Fawlty' also but at least you're not going to bash an innocent Spanish waiter over the head with a frying pan'!!

I consulted my bank once why some funds had not shown up on my account when they said 'it was a bouncing cheque'...........I retorted 'Patrik Berger on a trampolene is a 'bouncing Czech' also but at least he'll not effect my ability to meet commitments to direct debits'!!

A few years back I saw Ian Woosnam get very angry at the British Open...........I turned and said to my dad 'what's wrong with him'...........he replied 'he had a club too many in his bag'...........I responded 'Marcus Bent has had a 'club too many' also but at least that Welsh guy still has a chance of going on to win something'!!

After the 2008 Champions League Final between Man U and Chelsea, when John Terry missed that penalty, my cousin said 'he bottled it'...........I quipped 'the guy who discovered Perrier water 'bottled it' also but at least he only went on to drink it as opposed to slipping on it aswell'!!

My cousin crashed his car one time when he described the vehicle as being a 'write off'...........I tried to humour him by joking 'when I saw an Arsenal centre forward called Ian receiving a red card that was a 'Wright off' also but at least you could give the thing a good kicking without getting into further trouble'!!

I heard a guy on BBC News 24 during April 2010 say that Tiger Woods, after his personal problems, was back in the 'public gaze'..........I turned to my dad and quipped 'Elton John and George Michael are 'public gays' also and come to think of it golfers don't want the sun to go down on them either'!!

I also heard on BBC News 24 during the run up to the general election in the U.K. of May, 2010 that some people were prepared to throw some 'weight behind' a party...........I turned to my dad and said 'it doesn't surprise me as, because the British are queues mad, that somebody would be a proponent of 'wait behind' somebody'!!

I was talking to a friend of mine one day when he confidently boasted, because he had been playing so well, that he would shoot a really tough hole we knew in 'par'..........I retorted 'if you shoot par for that hole 'St. Elmo's Fire' was recorded by John Triple-Bogey'!!!!!

It always makes me laugh when I see a football club with the word 'Athletic' as part of it's name...........for example a football club is hardly going to call itself Wigan Self-oppressed Emotional Dead-weights now are they??!!!!!

My partner asked me would I 'make the earth move' for her..........I replied 'platetectonics would 'make the earth move' for you also but if that happens you needn't expect me to put those shelves up for you again'!!

I once heard a Geordie say 'wor Jack's in the army'..........I turned to my dad and quipped 'wor jack's in the bathroom with the shower and hand basin but while he was educated all about D-day we've educated ourselves about how to use a bidet'!!

I was watching Shamrock Rovers versus Bohemians at the beginning of April 2010 when, after the final whistle, the scorer of the winning goal i.e. Dennehy, bent over to catch his breath and all you could see was his ass..........the commentator simultaneously said he was now 'very much a HOOP'..........needless to say I thought it was amusing enough to write this joke!!!!!

I was listening to 'Boogie Nights' on Dublin 's Q102 during April 2010 when the deejay i.e. Lisa Armstrong said 'we have Toni Basil's 'Mickey' on the way'..........I thought 'do you not have her ass and her titties on the way too, no??'!!

After the Scottish Cup semi-final during April 2010 in which Ross County defeated Celtic their manager, Derek Adams, said 'they had played Celtic off the park'..........I turned to my dad and said "maybe that's why they won..........Celtic were probably expecting them to play them ON the park'!!

I was watching R.T.E. news once when I heard a policeman, regarding their investigation into a crime, say they weren't 'ruling anything out'..........I turned to my dad and reacted 'a carpenter who has just been laid off won't be 'ruling anything out' either but at least he doesn't go around beating people with a four-be-four baton'!!

I heard on the radio one day that the Lotto had 'rolled over more than ten times'..........I turned to one of my mates and said 'Demis Roussos on top of Mount Everest would 'roll over more than ten times' also but what you would then have is a snowball large enough that it actually would stand a chance in Hell'!!

They say 'fools and their money are parted easily'..........well I knew someone who was so mean he could possibly be diagnosed as being a genius...........Shirley Bassey should re-record 'Hey, Big Spender' and re-name it 'Hey, Big Miser'...........this guy could balance the books on top of The Spire without the need for a creditors ledger...........he wanted to become a classical music journalist so he could take and listen to 'notes'..........this bloke doesn't come into money, he multiple orgasms into it'!!!!!

I also heard on the radio one day that Bernard Dunne 'felt pressure in the ring'..........I turned to one of the lads and quipped 'when I ate prunes after drinking stout I 'felt pressure in the ring' also but at least this boxer wore a gum-shield for just boxing and not for gnashing his teeth because his 'ring' was a tap'!!

I'm approaching my forties and chatted up a young girl who told me when I came on to her 'you're too old'...........I retorted 'I'm about as old as YOUNG McDonald who had a farm and can't even get a beer served to him if he's not in possession of his driver's licence.....eeh ay eeh ay oh'!!

I was watching football when a player got sent off for a series of tackles which the commentator said 'he got his just deserts'...........I commented 'when I turned up late for a 4-course meal I got 'just desserts' also but at least, unlike the ball player, I was a 'trifle' lucky'!!

My dad got gas installed in the family home and one of the stickers put up by the fitters read 'If you smell gas at home'...........I thought it funny if you were to punctuate this sentence to read 'If you smell, gas at home'..........in other words 'If you are a bean eater, you needn't fart while out in public'!!!!!

One day my beloved Liverpool lost a big game that devastated me which motivated my dad to say 'keep your chin up'..........I humorously retorted 'a forty stone bloke from Beijing wearing a polar neck 'keeps his Chin up' also but at least my depression isn't going to make me gorge on Cornish pasties and cheeseburgers with mayonnaise'!!

I once went for a job interview when my mam said 'I'll keep my fingers crossed'..........I quipped 'when the pianist with The Boomtown Rats played out-side right 'Johnny Fingers crossed' on a number of occasions also but at least he was in a stronger position to negotiate a contract on improved terms for himself'!!

I used to drink stout when one day a bad barman gave me a pint full of gas..........when I complained his response was 'it's just a few bubbles'..........I hit back by retorting 'if I wanted 'bubbles' I'd have invited Michael Jackson's pet monkey in a Wonderbra whilst eating an Aero around'!!

My uncle once talked to me about World War II when he mentioned the 'Graveyard Shift'...........I responded 'when I kissed my ex-girlfriend up in St. Fintan's cemetary that was a 'graveyard shift' also but I bet they never got to fondle a pair of melon boobs in the process'!!!!!

One of my mates told me that after eating a dodgy curry he took laxitives as he wanted to 'get it out of his arseh*le'...........I humorously quipped 'when my car broke down in rural Carlow I wanted to get it out of 'the arseh*le' also for fear, because of the Dublin registration plate, it would be set upon by some culchies wielding hurley sticks'!!!!!

I once heard a preacher on The God Channel describe somebody as 'back-sliding'..........I turned to my girlfriend and said 'let's make love on grease-proof paper covered in cooking oil so that you'll be 'back-sliding' also but at least then we'll have something to cover our bun in the oven with'!!

I saw during April 2010 that Liverpool Football Club were 'up for sale'..........I thought 'rugby fans in Manchester are usually 'up for Sale' also but if the new owners were to come in and think they could get away with chanting 'you Scouse b*stard' they'd be run out of Merseyside'!!

I was in the pub one night when one of the lads commented that Barcelona's home ground, because of it's name, was a bit gay..........I quipped 'while Graham Norton is the New Camp, Quentin Crisp is his tent with Lord Baden Powell and some boy scouts is the Old Camp, ey??'!!

I was watching Bayern Munich versus Lyon in the Champions League semi-final during April 2010 when yer man Cris off Lyon went up for a header and came down heavily on his lower back..........one of my mates said, because of what was on the base of his spine, 'he came down on his tatoo'..........I quipped 'when rain fell on Fantasy Island it came down on Tatoo also but at least the French guy was not a short arse, squeeky little munchkin'!!

My girlfriend once said that, that 'ground control is very effective'..........I replied 'when Steven Gerrard plays football, because of his first touch, he has very effective 'ground control' also but at least, unlike air traffic controllers, ah Stevie has lifted the European Cup'!!!!!

While watching the 2008 Champions League final in Moscow between Chelsea and Man U John Terry was caught calling Carlos Tevez 'a facking Argie cant'..........I turned to my dad and said 'there was a guy called Cant who was on the B.B.C. 20-30 years ago but at least all he wanted to do was 'Play Away' as opposed to curse away'!!

I asked my girlfriend where I could find the beer we bought when she replied 'in the cooler'..........I quipped 'Steve McQueen when acting in The Great Escape was 'in The Cooler' on a few occasions also but if he ended up with a beverage that was as flat as your chest it wouldn't have been just the baseball that hit the roof'!!

I had an argument with my girlfriend when a pal of mine advised that we should just 'kiss and make up'..........I humorously retorted 'when I saw the video for 'Crazy, Crazy Nights' that was 'Kiss and make-up' also but at least the only time we stick our tongues out is when we are French snogging'!!

I was once told that a memory test invented by boy scouts was referred to as 'Kim's game'..........I responded 'golf is 'Anthony Kim's game' but when he plays eighteen he doesn't sit around camp-fires saying dib-dib-dib'!!

I heard on Sky Sports during an important Man U game at the end of April 2010 that 'the stakes were high'..........I turned to one of my mates and commented 'when Argentinians cook their meat in The Andes 'the steaks were high' also but at least the Red Devils are only interested in covering themselves in glory as opposed to pepper sauce'!!

My dad told me one day that a product that meets quality standards has a 'kitemark'..........I quipped 'an American golfer whose ball pitches on the green makes a 'Tom Kite mark' but I wouldn't say anyone in the British Standards Institution is a ringer for Nikki Lauda'!!

My late mother was reading a book one day when I asked her what it was..........she said 'it's a good story called 'From Here To Eternity' which is set in Hawaii'..........I responded 'when I die I'll be going from here to eternity also but at least in heaven I'll have little chance of bumping into someone saying 'book him Dano'!!!!!

I was watching a television programme on Chinese industrialisation which was called 'The Great Leap Forward'..........I turned to my late mother and quipped 'when Bob Beamon broke the world record for the long jump that was a great leap forward also but at least he didn't go on about egg flied lice'!!!!!

I was once asked if I knew that a cash register was called a 'Jewish piano'..........I quipped 'Jesus Christ could have played a 'Jewish piano' also but he's more concerned with having 'keys' to Hades'!!

I saw on the business news on R.T.E. that some company made a 'share offer'..........I thought to myself 'when the artist who recorded 'The Shoop, Shoop Song' invited me around for dinner that was a 'Cher offer' also but when she wanted to know if I loved her so I told her to kiss my ass'!!

I was talking to a guy who commented regarding betting that 'hindsight is a wonderful thing'..........to which I replied 'when Jim Kerr walked two thousand miles through the snow one Christmas time to have his marriage proposal accepted 'Chrissie Hynde's sight' was a wonderful thing also but when she looked back she probably thought she could have run to the bookies and put some money on it happening beforehand'!!

I heard on the news one day that a guy was released from prison because his conviction was overturned to which my dad said 'he must have 'lost the plot' with such an injustice'..........I quipped 'because the British still rule in Northern Ireland the Taigs have also 'lost the plot.......... of land that is, but if you were to say Tiocfaidh Ar La in London they'd probably think you were one of The Guildford Four'!!

I once learned that there is a play called 'The Lady's Not For Burning' which is all about witchcraft..........I thought to myself 'Joan Of Arc's parents probably appealed that 'the lady's not for burning' also but it wasn't long before they were dialling 999 for the fire brigade, was it??'!!

I was once told that Margaret Thatcher was nicknamed 'the lady with the blow lamp'..........I quipped 'when a bloke I know had his scrotum painted with Hammerite on his stag night his future wife was a 'lady with a blow lamp' also but nobody would have begrudged her if she had decided to 'privatise' his privates or cover his genitals with a drainpipe before he went on the p*ss with his so-called mates'!!

A telephone call was made to my moblie, which I had left behind me in a coffee shop which some yuppie picked up, when I asked him who the caller was he just fobbed me off and said 'Joe Bloggs'..........I hit back by retorting 'well I'm sure Joe e-mails and texts also but I'd say he put a whole tub of Brylcreem in his hair at one go'!!

It is often said when a nation is at war that, because they must choose between arming and feeding themselves, it's 'guns or butter'..........I thought to myself 'when Marlon Brando had to choose between acting in 'The Godfather' and 'Last Tango In Paris' that was 'guns or butter' also but at least when you shoot movies you don't come up against evil dictators who'll not compromise what they put on their toast'!!!!!

I was having a laugh with one of my mates when I quipped that Ashley 'Coal' had near relations called 'peas and beans'..........I continued 'maybe he's also related to the son of perdition'..........when he asked why I continued 'because opposed to being called the antichrist he might well be the anthracite that's why ya fecking eejit'!!!!!

My dad told me that Peter Sellers was in a comedy called 'The Ladykillers'..........I quipped 'the recorders of the song 'Human' in blouses, skirts and polka dot tights could be 'Lady-Killers' also and come to think of it, it would be just as funny a thought as 'The Pink Panther'!!

An Australian told me that his musical instrument was called a 'jingling Johnnie'..........I responded 'Mates condoms with bells could be referred to as being 'jingling johnnies' also but I suppose that implement is such a passion killer it would be as useful as contraception itself'!!

I once heard somebody say that AIDS is called 'gay plague'...........my friend asked 'that's just like the black death, right'..........I added 'when there was civil war in Rwanda back in the Nineties there was plenty of 'black death' there also but at least they didn't have naked posters of Ru Paul hanging up in their bedrooms'!!!!!

My friend told me he saw some guy 'knock seven bells' out of some other guy..........I humorously continued 'Quasi Modo whilst drinking out of his beer 'bong' used to knock seven bells out at Notre Dame Cathedral also but when he did it meant he was an hour late for The Angelus'!!!!!

I once heard a smug and pretentious female saying 'here in California everyone is so organised, we have our ducks in row'..........I turned to my girlfriend and said 'I remember Viv Richards going a whole Test Series without scoring any runs thus he had several 'ducks' in a row also but at least he only wants to chill with real people and drink 'Malibu' as opposed to living there'!!!!!

My girlfriend said to me once, when I got home from the pub, I was 'in the doghouse'..........I retorted 'the blokes who work in the I.S.P.C.A. are always 'in the doghouse' also but at least they are not fearful of having another snake bite'!!

I once heard on Sky Sports News that Carlo Ancelotti was 'in the frame' for the Manager Of The Month Award..........I turned to my dad and said 'the Mona Lisa is always 'in the frame' also but at least it's obvious that that Italian guy has at least one eyebrow'!!

My friend said to me that Los Angeles is called La La Land...........I responded 'a teletubby in Liverpool could be in 'la la land' also but when he has a few on him instead of saying 'yo dude' he'd say 'come 'ead yer friggin' beer monsteh, say ay oh whack"!!

My mate also once told me that the warm ocean temperatures in equatorial Pacific are called 'El Nino'...........I quipped 'Liverpool fans called Fernando Torres 'El Nino' also but the weather cannot guarantee you 30 goals a season nor 50 million euros in the transfer market'!!

I think Amanda Brunker is the sexiest woman alive..........not only does she float my boat but she floats my entire fleet, heavy laden with lead!!

After what Liverpool fans did at Heysel in 1985 the game was never going to go our way..........the referee denied us everything..........I mean Ronnie Whelan was hacked down for a penalty that was not only 'stonewall' but actually The Great Wall Of China plus the building boom during The Celtic Tiger!!

 I once heard an American student describe sex as 'knock boots'..........I retorted 'when The Blessed Virgin showed up in the west of Ireland wearing Doc Martins they could be described as being 'Knock boots' also but there's obviously no way you could claim to an 'Immaculate Conception'!!

I heard 'Willie Thorne' say during the World Snooker Championship of 2010 that a player had 'over-screwed on a few occasions'..........I turned to one of the lads and continued 'a retired nymphomaniac who participated in group sex has 'over-screwed on a few occasions' also I suppose but I wouldn't say her name sounds like she'd took out her manhood while amongst some berry bushes'!!

A mate of mine said about a guy we dislike that 'he's a pr*ck with ears'..........I humorously added 'not only is he a pr*ck with ears but the ears have ear-rings of pr*cks on them also'!!

I saw an add for a spot remover that said it 'tries to remove redness'..........I turned to my girlfriend and said 'before you go to the gym after I've spanked you with a snorkling flipper, you 'try to remove redness' also but at least with a spot on your face you can cover it with make up'!!

While watching the news I heard the newsreader describe that someone had 'jumped the gun'..........I quipped 'the lady who slept with Magnum P.I. 'jumped the gun' also but at least she dressed in something other than Hawaiian shirts'!!

Whilst watching a sports programme I heard the presenter say that, regarding Grimsby Town's survival hopes, that they were 'staying alive'..........I turned to my girlfriend and commented 'The Bee Gees had a hit called 'Staying Alive' also but when the footballers socialise I wouldn't say they could dance as well as John Travolta in 'Saturday Night Fever'..........and come to think of it, because Grimsby is a fishing town, instead of a sea 'bass' on the end of the line the song has a serious 'bass' line!!

Yet again, while watching the World Snooker Championship in 2010 I heard the commentator saying that a player got a 'good kick'..........I quipped to my dad 'when a poor unfortunate mugged a hard lad I know's mam he ended up getting a 'good kick-ing' also but at least in snooker the players fill the pockets as opposed to emptying out those they are not welcome to'!!

I heard on Sky News' business section one day that a company, in order to raise money for a takeover, issued a 'junk bond'..........I thought 'Steptoe & Son have a 'junk bond' also but at least on Sky News you'll not see a horse called Hercules sh*t in The City'!!

I was talking to a girl I know when she said about her boyfriend, regarding his vulnerability 'I'll have him where I want him'..........I quipped 'the day Osama Bin Laden is captured you'll 'have him where you want him' also but at least your boyfriend isn't hiding himself in caves along the Afghan-Pakistan border plotting his next terror activity'!!

My mate said 'we should go to a strip club to see some pole dancing'..........I retorted humorously 'socialise with Artur Boruc the evening of an Old Firm triumph and you'll see some 'Pole dancing', with delight that is, also but at least he'll not proceed to bend over and spank his own ass'!!

My sister was watching a film when I asked her what it was..........she replied ''A High Wind In Jamaica'', it has pirates in it'..........I quipped 'Brian Lara smoking marijuana after eating beans could be 'a high wind in Jamaica' also but, unlike Long John Silver, when he's 'stumped' he doesn't hope back to the pavillion with a parrot on his shoulder'!!!!!

I was watching a crime programme where it was mentioned that some people were on a criminals 'hit list'............I turned to my dad and said 'U2 have a 'hit list' also but the only time anyone's life was in danger was when they played 'Bullet The Blue Sky'!!!!!

I heard a journalist once describe Pakistan as a terrorist 'hot spot'..........I turned to my girlfriend and said 'if you were to put prunes through a vindaloo your arseh*le would be a 'hot spot' also but at least if you were to wipe it nobody in the Middle East would take offence to a Japanese flag'!!

During the episode when there was that volcanic eruption in Iceland during April 2010 I heard a person say 'the geyser must have blew up'..........I turned to one of the lads and said 'when I kicked a Cockney in the goolies 'the geyser blew up' also but at least he didn't disrupt flights throughout the whole of northern Europe'!!

My girlfriend said to me that she had bought some great tickets for a play that she described as being 'in the front row'..........I quipped 'a hooker in rugby is 'in the front row' also but I suppose we'll not have to worry about somebody in the second row putting his arm through our legs and grabbing us by the shorts'!!

I heard during the run up to the general election in the U.K. of 2010 that 'victory spurs them on'..........I thought 'Tottenham fans in cowboy boots is what 'Spurs' their team on to victory also but at least politicians don't have to worry about Chas & Dave writing songs about them'!!

My sister asked was I aware of the book 'I Know Why The Caged Bird Sings'..........I answered 'the inmates of Prisoner Cell Block H at a football match could be 'caged birds singing' also but at least most sports fans eat and don't do porridge'!!

I learned that knowledge within the stock exchange was referred to as 'insider dealing'..........I thought 'a guy who invites his mates around for a game of poker is an example of 'insider dealing' also but at least your mates cannot be regarded as bulls and bears'!!

On the sports news one day I heard the deejay say that a player had 'given the lead' to his team..........I said to my partner 'when I didn't want to walk the dog you were 'given the lead' also but at least footballers don't have to worry about picking up canine sh*t so as not to be an offence to others'!!

Yet again, during the World Snooker Championship of 2010 I heard the commentator say contact between two balls was 'a little too thick'..........I thought ' a guy I went to school with who only got 15 points in his Leaving Cert back in 1990 was 'a little too thick' to even gets Arts in U.C.D. but at least, unlike what they say about good snooker players, going on to study theology isn't a sign of a mis-spent youth'!!

During another game of snooker I heard the commentator say that a player 'was looking for a plant'..........I thought 'when the police's drug unit searched a Rastafarians home for marijuana they 'were looking for a plant' or two also but, unlike ambitious snooker players, the people in the flat above were letting the 'grass' grow beneath their feet'!!

My cousin was listening to heavy metal when I asked him what it was..........he said 'hard rock'..........I replied 'Jesus Christ drinking beer with Biffa Bacon could be referred to as being 'hard Rock' also but at least you'll not be betrayed by your 'Judas' Priest'!!!!!

I was at a wedding where I had a choice of starters when my cousin said 'take the soup'..........I quipped 'when Protestants convert to Roman Catholicism they 'take the soup' also but let's hope that at least when the happy couple have their differences they don't re-enact the Battle Of The Boyne'!!

I've also learned that a theatre production with dancing girls is called a 'leg show'..........I thought 'Premier League Darts could be referred to as being a 'leg show' also but darts fans are more turned on by the level of attention on the 'lipstick'!!

My dad once described two of his friends as 'joined at the hip'..........I responded 'Siamese twins who decide to become prostitutes are 'joined at the hip' also but at least when your friends get together it cannot be described as being a fearsome foursome'!!

I was told that when the Enola Gay dropped the atomic bomb on Hiroshima it was phrased that it had 'dropped little boy'..........I quipped 'when Anthea Turner broke off her relationship to Bruno Brookes she 'dropped little boy' also and come to think of it the little fecker probably blew up just like the bomb itself'!!

My mate told me that aliens are called 'little green men'..........I retorted 'because I am subject to a lot of jealousy and envy I feel I'm surrounded by 'little green men' also but if I was to say this to them they'd probably try to turn the tables on me by labelling me a 'space cadet' of my own'!!

I learned that crown prince Wilhelm of Prussia was nicknamed 'Little Willie'..........I thought 'Mark Owen out of 'Take That' said some years back that he had a 'little willie' also and I suppose it wasn't long afterwards that he was trying to 'Rule The World' aswell, was it??'!!

I've learned that Roman Catholics are called 'left footers'..........I thought 'Diego Maradona is a left footer also but his most famous goal was actually scored with 'The Hand Of God'!!

My mate said to me that a religious cult involved in trying to recruit new members practice 'love bombing'...........I humorously replied 'Al-Qaeda 'love bombing' also but at least they promise that you'll be able to have sex with a load of virgins when you become a martyr for them'!!

On another occasion I heard a person describe a pregnant lady as being 'in the club'...........I thought to myself 'a guy with a short leg putting it's prosthetic end on a big soled boot is putting it 'in the club' also but at least he doesn't have a craving for strawberry jam on pizzas'!!

I read in the newspaper about a guy who left his wife for another woman being referred to as a 'love rat'...........I thought 'Michael Jackson wrote a song about a 'love rat' also but at least it was affectionately called 'Ben' as opposed to domineeringly instructing 'Ben-d over'!!

Billy Davies said during the week in the run up to the Championship play-offs of 2010 that a manager who gets his team up to the Premiership 'should have an 18 month sack free zone'...........I thought 'The Women's Institute is a 'sack free zone' also but maybe Billy could hide his goolies in the 'bags' beneath his eyes, ey??'!!

Sarah Jessica Parker said during May 2010, regarding her work colleagues, that they have a 'common bond'...........I said to my mate '007 in a tracksuit and cheap gold jewellery is a 'common Bond' also but while Sarah and her friends go in search of 'Sex & The City' he looks about for 'Pussy Galore'!!

I was watching The Player's Championship at Sawgrass during May 2010 when Butch Harmon said the greens were 'hard and fast'..........I turned to my dad and quipped 'Usain Bolt with a flick knife is 'hard and fast' but you might actually go on to win the tournament if you can Jamaica putt or two, ey??'!!

I also saw a guy called Van Pelt playing in the same tournament..........I commented to my brother-in-law 'when the P.S.N.I. drive around, Republicans 'van pelt' with rocks and petrol bombs also but at least the golfer knows how to treat 'greens', ey??'

I heard Fergie from Black Eyed Peas sing about her 'lovely lady lumps' in one of their songs..........I thought 'breast cancer are 'lady lumps' also which, unlike the song, actually do make 'Big Girls' cry'!!

My friend said to me that the electric chair is called 'the hot squat'..........I quipped 'a female urinating in the desert could be referred to as a 'hot squat' also but at least when you go to the toilet it wouldn't have been after you've spent ten years on death row'!!!!!

I've learned that Johnny Adair is nicknamed 'Mad Dog'..........I thought 'fill Lassie's bowl with bleach and you'd have a 'mad dog' also but while the film title asks her to 'Come Home', this loyalist has been well and truly ordered to stay in Great Britain'!!

I asked my late mother what she was watching on television one time when she replied 'it's a kitchen sink drama'..........I responded 'when I watched Liverpool apply pressure for a winning goal a while back, because of what they threw at the opposition, that could have been described as being a 'kitchen sink drama' also but at least at the end of the game, because they had succeeded, it was only our opponents that were left feeling 'drained'!!

My friend once told me that conservative views are referred to as 'hard hat'..........I quipped 'the puppets in Fraggle Rock could also be referred to as being 'hard hat' but at least they didn't have the Irish government during the property boom trying to simultaneously make 'muppets' out of them'!!!!!

A friend of mine once said to me because that p*ss Breo was only out for a short time that it could be referred to as 'guest beer'..........I quipped 'Liza Minnelli's ex-husband's urine sample after a few pints could be referred to as 'Guest beer' also but at least when a beer tap lets the beer flow it doesn't have to worry about more that two shakes being regarded as a w*nk'!!!!!

I heard on the news that the police regarded a bank robbery as an 'inside job'..........I thought 'a house cleaner does an 'inside job' also but at least they leave quietly and don't have to worry about CCTV and get away cars'!!

My partner said one night before going to bed 'let's make music together'..........I cheekily replied 'Slipknot 'make music together' also but if you expect me to put on a leather mask, whip my 'flute' out and piddle all over the place forget about it baby'!!

Before a football match I heard a commentator say that it was going to be 'some spectacle'..........I turned to one of the lads and said 'it would take 'some spectacle' to cover one of Mathieu Flamini's eyes but instead of going to AC Milan he may have been better off if he had 'gone to Specsavers' instead'!!

One day I was confronted by a fairly aggressive beggar when my mate said 'he was an up front bum'..........I quipped 'an Australian having sex with his partner shoves it 'up front-bum' also but at least with a beggar you still have the possibility of holding on to the contents of your wallet'!!

I heard a story about a guy who used to beat up his wife when he came home from the pub with a few drinks on him..........but one night he called to say that he would be home early to 'take her out'..........much to his astonishment when he got home his wife decided that she was going to 'take him out'..........with a rolling pin that is which saw to it that it was not just with drunkeness that he blacked out..........next day he had the sorest head he'd ever had!!

I was told that if you cause trouble you 'make waves'..........I thought 'earthquakes beneath the ocean 'make waves' also but I doubt very much that those at the shore would be glad that the surf was up'!!

I was also told that a teenager who hangs about shopping centres in the U.S. is called a 'mall rat'..........I thought 'Tiffany inflicting Weil's disease could be referred to being a 'mall rat' also but because her fans appear like lambs but breed like the vermin it was very wrong for her to 'think we're alone now', was it??'!!

I read on the teletext during May 2010 about a Celtic player who said he had 'made a name for himself'..........I thought 'when I entitled myself " Ah Cormo 'Blessed is he who comes in the name of the Scouse' Macker" I made a name for myself also so why didn't he do something similar by calling himself Niall McGinn 'n' Tonic for example, ey??'!!

I heard a commentator mention during a rugby league game that 'the hooter had gone'..........I thought 'a lady who has lost a breast due to cancer meant that 'the hooter had gone' also but at least at a rugby game you are not caught out if you go on to give birth to twins'!!

My mam said to me when I was very young not to cross the road 'until you see the green man flashing'..........I thought 'The Incredible Hulk wearing nothing but a trenchcoat is a green man flashing also but at least traffic lights don't have to worry about the size of their manhood during Winter'!!!!!

I once heard a football commentator describe a game that was certain to be won as being 'in the bag'..........I quipped to my partner 'testicles are 'in the bag' also but if they were involved in a kick-about it would mean excruciating pain'!!

In the run up to the 2010 general election in the U.K. Gordon Brown said 'I will do it my way'..........I turned to my dad and said 'Frank Sinatra said he'd do it 'My Way' also but at least he had two good Ol' Blue Eyes as opposed to one dodgy Brown one'!!!!!

I believe the garments that dancers have worn are called 'leg warmers'..........I thought 'incontinency is a 'leg warmer' also but most people who are this way are in their Eighties as opposed to being members of the Fame cast that emerged during this decade'!!

My girlfriend one day said that she hated cleaning the bedroom as she regarded it as 'grunt work'..........I quipped 'prostitution in Amsterdam is 'grunt work' also but at least when you clean up you don't have to worry about wearing a Dutch cap'!!!!!

 A mate of mine was on a diet and said 'I eat nothing after 4 p.m.'..........I quipped 'by not eating anything after 4 p.m. you eat something'..........very confusingly he replied 'what do you mean?'..........I humorously responded 'it's a paradox..........by not eating anything after 4 p.m. actually means you eat jack sh*t'!!!!!

While walking by a camp site my friend said 'they're all Roma gypsies in there'...........I responded 'how do you know...........just because they like football doesn't give you the right to assume what team they like...........they could be LAZIO gypsies for all you know..........come to think of it fans of Bohemians here in Dublin probably follow them'!!!!!

I asked my partner to wash the dishes as I said 'it's your turn'..........when she declined I quipped 'even if you were to drive to the beauticians you'd have to take some 'turns' also but come to think of it you are probably afraid of breaking a nail you'd rather stick into my back'!!

Apparently the Association of Tennis Professionals have told Steve Denton that they are going to give him an award for his 'services' to tennis...........but they've also told him that when it comes to his ground strokes, because they were so average, that he can go and f*ck himself!!

A mate of mine said to me that I look like John Saxon............ after google-ing to see what he looked like I came back to him and said 'Hey pal, I look nothing like him..........if I was his black, non-identical twin sister who was adopted I'd resemble him more'!!!!!

I was in the pub one night when one of my mates, who supports Chelsea, said about his team 'you won't beat Our Gang'..........I turned and said 'just because Jon Obi Mikel has hair like Buckwheat doesn't guarantee that you'll not have a leaky defence come the weekend'!!

Some of you may remember that group who were out in The Eighties, who one of my mates thought were funny, called Yello...........I quipped 'if Yello are funny so is an Oriental orphan alcoholic rent boy on a diet of nothing but sweetcorn with sclerosis of the liver'!!

A body-building member o f the Norn Irelint assembly with a prosthetic arm entered an angling competition when, on throwing the line into the water, it flew off and was set upon by a load of piranhas whose sh*t has apparently increased the PSNI's stockpile of plastic bullets ten fold!!!!!

Approaching the end of May 2010 I heard an advertisement on the radio where a guy said, regarding one of his sons, 'my middle fella's heavy'..........I thought 'Linford Christie's middle fella's heavy also but it sounds like this young guy ate a 'whole' ring of black pudding as opposed to the sprinter's wife who just got her 'hole' off it'!!